D1372621

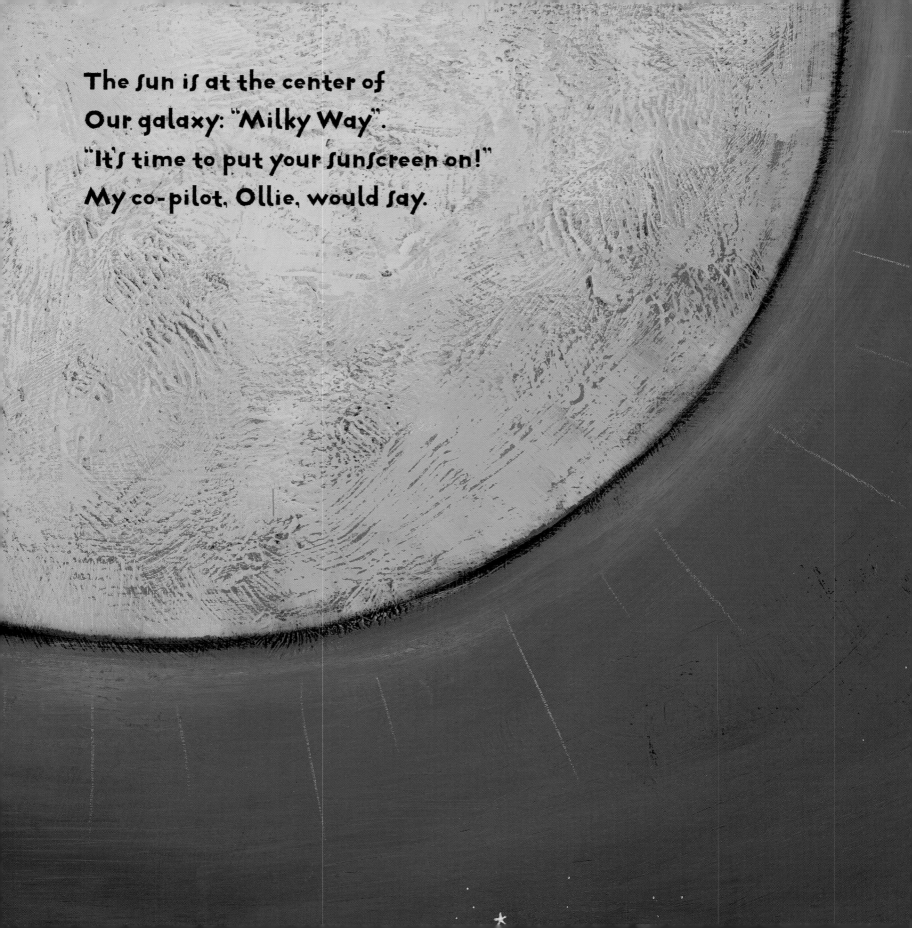

The sun is at the center of
Our galaxy: "Milky Way".
"It's time to put your sunscreen on!"
My co-pilot, Ollie, would say.

'Round and 'round the yellow sun
All the planets go—
From Mercury, our very first stop
All the way to Pluto.

Venus is the next in line.
It sure is dark and cloudy.
Ollie and I fly on by.
We wave and shout out "howdy!"

From here the Earth looks blue and green,
And like a little ball.
I think my friends are waving to me.
Wow! They look so small.

The Moon goes around our planet Earth.
Some say it's made of cheese.
Ollie picks up a little chunk.
The moon dust makes him sneeze!

Astronauts have walked right here.
It's pretty close to home.
They left a flag as a souvenir,
And isn't that a comb?

Mars is our next-door neighbor—
A planet bright and red.
Like Earth, it has mountains and valleys,
But it's very cold instead.

Since this is sort of like our home,
Some say there's life on Mars.
I think I'll take some pictures
Of their fancy Martian cars.

Jupiter has 16 moons–
That's an awful lot!
The biggest planet of them all
Is known for its "Great Red Spot".

What could be inside the spot
On Jupiter's windy face?
Polka-dot space kids at camp,
Having a three-legged race?

START

Let's take a trip around Saturn's rings.
They're made of ice and rock.
And outside Saturn's many rings
There's 21 moons to dock!

From here we see Uranus,
And its blue-green clouds so pale.
Our tour is almost over
Of our planetary trail.

Neptune is eighth and Pluto is ninth,
But Pluto hates losing races!
Nobody ever likes to be last,
So sometimes they switch places.

That's the end of our race into space.
Millions of miles we've gone.
But maybe it's time to get back into bed...
I think I'm starting to yawn!

I love exploring the Solar System!
It's such a fun place to roam.
But Ollie and I are glad to be back
'Cause Earth is our home sweet home!